There is nothing romantic about death

Banji Coker

Ukiyoto Publishing

All global publishing rights are held by

Ukiyoto Publishing

Published in 2023

Content Copyright © Banji Coker

ISBN 9789359200019

Edition 1

All rights reserved.

No part of this publication may be reproduced, transmitted, or stored in a retrieval system, in any form by any means, electronic, mechanical, photocopying, recording or otherwise, without the prior permission of the publisher.

The moral rights of the author have been asserted.

This is a work of fiction. Names, characters, businesses, places, events, locales, and incidents are either the products of the author's imagination or used in a fictitious manner. Any resemblance to actual persons, living or dead, or actual events is purely coincidental.

This book is sold subject to the condition that it shall not by way of trade or otherwise, be lent, resold, hired out or otherwise circulated, without the publisher's prior consent, in any form of binding or cover other than that in which it is published.

www.ukiyoto.com

Contents

Chapter 1	1
Chapter 2	16
Chapter 3	26
Chapter 4	31
Chapter 5	40
Chapter 6	47
Chapter 7	51
Chapter 8	56
Chapter 9	60
About the Author	65

Chapter 1

So you want to know about me? ever since I woke up here, everyone has been asking me questions about myself, you all think I am crazy and you feel something in my past will give you an insight as to why?

I am not sure about where to start from, but I think my 20th birthday might be a decent place to begin. I was standing in front of the mirror in my small cubical bathroom overwhelmed by the rushing sound of the shower and the soothing music from my phone playing in the background. My body started moving, void of my control and before I knew it, my vison began to go dim, I struggled to find my stance and also maintain my posture and within a few seconds everything went back to normal. This was not the first time, and what was more worrying was the fact that it happens at least once every year, on the day of my birth ever since I was 12.

When this happened the previous year, I told my mother, I was taken to a lab to test for malaria and typhoid, I think my mother prayed I tested positive for either one of these, because, her child's vision going dim for a few seconds was scary, but if malaria or typhoid could somehow take the blame for it, this would mean getting a medication of 2500 naira and no one especially her would have to suffer sleepless nights.

I tested positive for typhoid but I knew deep down it wasn't the cause of this, growing up with struggling parents especially when you know they have no idea what they are doing, you try your best not to be a burden. My parents sacrificed everything so I could have a comfortable life, they even stayed together because they were made to believe that children of divorce don't end up very well. I was constantly reminded of the things they did for me and some days it felt like my existence prevented them from achieving.

My parents never intended to get married to each other, my dad was 24 years old and still trying to figure his life out when he got my 21 years old mother pregnant. And because my grandparents were family friends who respected each other, a marriage was arranged.

2 There is nothing romantic about death

I was an expensive liability, they never said any of these to me but I could see it in my darkest days they wish they never had me, I was always falling sick, always reacting to something, and for a couple who weren't prepared to get married or have kids, it was frustrating. When I was 8 my dad came home jobless, the day before, he was a young managing director of one of the foremost banks in the country and as it was the custom of banks around that time, it was declared insolvent, making and leaving people who lost their money and jobs in the process of the closure bitter and hopeless. It was in that year my parents had one of their biggest fights, I can't remember what their fight was about all I remember was I ended up spending 3 years in my grandma's house away from them.

During that 3 years period, my mother's small supermarket was bulldozed by the government on claims that it was on a land which was commissioned for the building of roads, no compensation was made to my mother by the government and thankfully enough I wasn't with my parents to witness the toxic reaction that loss would have caused.

By the time I returned home, my parents had already found Jesus and life was filled with vigils, fasting , prayers, and scriptural blackmails. My parents had a lot to deal with and I tried my best not to add to their burden, I remember hiding in my room and holding my breath just to see if I would turn invisible. This is why I never told them about the reoccurrence of this thing, I will rather die than make anyone lose sleep over me.

For my parents, love was providing for your physical needs, flogging you to make sure you behave properly, and to them all these were supposed to make you happy, and if it didn't , they panicked and got defensive, phrases like "you're such an ungrateful child", "do you know how many people will kill to be in your shoes?" were thrown around. Children weren't born with 'how to manuals' and you can't give what you don't have, if the parents are broken so will the child, Just look at me.

I don't have a problem with how I was raised, I had it better than most, I was flogged but never physically abused, I didn't go hungry, I had food, I just didn't believe in anything except for the fact that everyone was sad about something. I didn't have the luxury of fairytales, not that I didn't get to watch Disney, but while Hollywood was trying to sell me make believe, reality didn't let me sleep. When I was 10, my parents were having a shouting match on one of their visits to see me at my grandma's, they dared each other to file for divorce, the phrase 'I will take my child and leave you' was flying around from both sides and I remember thinking how was I going to ensure I don't hurt one parent's feeling by choosing the other because individually they were decent at parenting but together they were a disaster.

I drew up a time table of how I would share my time with them when they got divorced, my dad looked at my time table and just said "Jesus doesn't like divorce and your mother won't make me sin against God" 10 years later they are still together with a marriage full of regrets and resentment.

You know I don't live with my parents anymore right?, and no, my parents did not kick me out, I am in transition, testing the adult waters, seeing if I am ready to start my life, and if it doesn't work out there is always the option of turning back and returning to my father's house.

My parents weren't big on my decision to move, pessimism and bitterness are eager viruses, they refuse to stay in just one host and demands to be passed from one person to another. "This freedom that you're so eager to experience, *shey* you know it's hard out there?" my mother asked when I told them about my plans for the third time, " you're an *ajebutter*, Lagos will eat you up in one minute". and yes their pessimism started to creep into me, Lagos is the land of opportunities but it was also the land that killed my parents dreams and made them into miserable human beings.

I got a job at this struggling publication because I didn't think I could get anything better, I was a fresh UNI graduate with no experience, I was lucky to even get a job in a city that expects you to have a 5 years worth of experience and not be over 22. I think getting the job and moving in with Tola were some of the things that prompted my parents into accepting the idea of me leaving the house.

"guy are you not going to work *ni*?!" Tola called out to me as I came out of the bathroom still feeling a little bit off balance. Tola and I have been friends since we were 12, our relationship has an embarrassing beginning, we were both in JSS 2 when we met, my parents had decided that a firm disciplinary school was a good fit for me. The school was owned by a retired military officer who missed his life in the army so much that he treated us like we were new recruits instead of students and ran the school as if it was a military training camp. We would always run to school once we could see the building, if anyone was caught walking, they were seriously disciplined with sticks. We were not to be caught outside our classes before or after recess, we were not to come out of our classes even if it was just to go to the toilet, there were patrol officers who made sure we didn't default, but still, students sneaked around.

The day before Tola and I became friends, some students were caught outside after recess, they were made into scapegoats, they were beaten in front of the whole school, screaming for their mothers, some even prayed to die. The next day, the day Tola and I became friends, I forgot to go to the toilet during recess and 4 hours before the end of school, I became pressed, sweating and trying to hold the pee that was begging to be released from my bladder, my body betrayed me, I wetted myself. Tola who was sitting close to me and had just transferred to the school a week before noticed, and instead of making a noise, he covered up for me, he poured his bottled water on my shorts and also on the place I had soiled, making it look like the liquid on my short and the floor was a clumsy mistake.

I was never really outgoing or friendly but every time we came in contact, I was extra, I tried repaying him for his kindness, I felt the need to free myself from being indebted to him, I couldn't have another person who like my parents spend every minute of my life reminding me of what they have done for me. But, he never gave me a reason to feel like I had to repay him, the feeling of indebtment quickly faded and we have been friends ever since.

With his neatly ironed shirt, he was ready to get to work, the reason my parents agreed to let me set out on my own, was become I was staying with someone familiar, someone who they considered to be more mature. Despite our deep friendship, Tola is quite different from me, Tola was every parents dream, the star pupil, he knew what parents wanted to see and presented himself that way, he dressed smart, he was articulate and handsome, and it wasn't only parents that fell for his charm, girls our age did too, I grew up being perceived as his awkward side-kick, always lost in his shadow, but the perception of others didn't sip into our relationship, we allowed each other to be our separate self, and years after, during our struggles in our separate universities, we appreciated our friendship, a relationship that allowed you be whatever you wanted to be unapologetically.

"I am going *oo*, I'm not just inspired" I replied still feeling a little hazy, it take me a bit of time before I fully recover from my mild blackouts.

"what time are you even supposed to resume *sef*?"

"by 8"

"you know its already 8 right?"

"yes, I will go there and now start writing stories about other people's lives"

"why don't you just quit since you hate it, *abi* your father still gives you allowance"

"I am not at home because I have a job, if I quit I don't have a reason to be away from home"

"Anyways, I am already leaving, me *sef* I am late for work" Tola said as he stepped out of the house.

By the way, please forgive my manners, my name is Oluwole and don't worry about my age or my last name, you probably have it in one of those files you guys keep, but if not, I want to be detailed and as well vague as much as possible, don't want anyone tracking me, I know your promise of confidentiality is actually shit.

So back to where we left off, I was 15 steps away from the street where I stay, when this guy approached me, looking rough and disoriented, I was about to distance myself when words started coming out of his mouth "sorry excuse me, please I am from Accra, I brought goods from Accra, electronics, phones, iPhones and I have people that want to purchase, they said I should meet them at Moshalashi busstop, please where is there?

looking a bit confused, I replied, "this is Moshalashi Bus stop"

There is nothing romantic about death

"*Abeg*, please can you follow me to where I put my goods, I don't understand Nigerian money and I don't want them to cheat me, I will give you money and a phone"

This was my first time having an actual conversation with someone who claimed to be a foreigner, I had meet several foreigners, but I never had any conversations. Western media never reports anything good about my country except when it comes to Afrobeats, when Nigeria is talked about, it's always about the Nigerian prince scams and corruption, South Africans don't like us either, their media is always branding us as rapists, and sex and drug traffickers.

So I thought being friendly with this Ghanaian man will at least help him see something positive about Nigeria, also, my eagerness to assist him was influenced by my desire to visit Ghana for an holiday. Maybe relating with someone from there will give me a feel of what to expect when I finally visit. But my good intentions didn't last very long, I almost overlooked this man's accent, he didn't sound Ghanaian, he wasn't adding "er" at the end of everything he said. I was in a hurry, but the fact that he was offering to pay me and also his very familiar accent which sounded Nigerian was feeding my skepticism, Lagos is not exactly a place of honesty, it is a jungle, where everyone is a predator and a prey.

The first thing that came to my mind was, if this man isn't being truthful, then he must be a kidnapper. what the hell did he mean by he doesn't understand Nigerian money, its just simple math, there is no special arithmetic attached to our currency, eventually, I decided to ditch him because of my skepticism, I rather be a terrible person than be a dead person .

"I am late for work, you can ask one of those *maruwa* drivers, maybe they can help" I said as I led him to a particular *maruwa* driver

"*Ejo* sir, he said he is from Ghana and he is looking for Moshalashi Bus stop.." before I could continue, the Ghanaian was already explaining himself. Shocked by the fact that he added Yoruba in his explanation, I figured I should be on my way, At least if his story was true, his understanding of Yoruba meant he wasn't exactly helpless after all, he could easily communicate with anyone and the guilt that was beginning to bug me slowly faded.

I was later than usual so I had to hurry, but before I could take my third step, the *maruwa* driver reached out for me and pulled me back, while I struggled myself out of his grip, he said "*egbon*, let us help him, you know we don't know tomorrow, we might need help and we will want someone to help us, let us just do it for God" I found the anxiousness in his voice very scary, why exactly was he so concerned? and why did he need me to join him in helping the guy?,

" I am already late for work"

"me too I have work, but let's help him, we too we will need help in the future" he said as he repeatedly looked back to trade glances with the Ghanaian man and before I could give my response he had turned towards him.

That was my cue, that was my out and just like someone troubled by his bowels I rushed towards the other direction as fast as my feet would carry me.

I won't lie, I was scared, I am not very street smart, I am what people call '*omo get* inside' growing up I was never allowed out of the house and for the most part of my childhood up to this point my parents did a pretty good job from sheltering me from the outside world.

This was my first experience being truly alone, I was scared of everything and everybody, I think that's what happens when you grow up around people suffering from PTSD, the fear gets genetic.

All through the day, I tried to reconcile my actions with my conscience, what exactly was I frightened about? I wondered if the Ghanaian man was really honest with his story and just needed help, but then again, this is Lagos, a place where being nice to a total stranger might get you robbed, kidnapped or killed, I tried my best to convince myself I did the right thing, Lagos does this to you, it takes away your ability to trust and gives you paranoia in return. We grew up hearing terrible stories and if we aren't careful some of us might end up having those stories as our reality.

When I got back home, I narrated the whole incident to my friend and his sister, before I could finish, Temi, Tola's younger sister jumped at my story and told us how she was in a similar situation and got robbed off all her belongings, according to her, both the Ghanaian man and the *maruwa* driver were partners and they were thieves , the whole thing was planned, they made sure they positioned themselves in such a position in which that particular *maruwa* driver was the one I would take him to, and I made the right choice by leaving.

I spent the night convincing myself that I did right thing, but that day wouldn't be the only time I would see the Ghanaian man, after that day, he became a prominent figure in my entire existence, might be the main reason I am even here.

~

The next day, cold sipped into my chest, the blanket I was laying on couldn't prevent me from feeling the hardness of the floor, because Tola and I were so eager to grow up, we had to do away with some of the comforts we grew up with, we already paid a year's rent before we realizing we had to pay for beds and furniture too, my crappy job wasn't paying enough and neither was Tola's. But it was our apartment so we were grateful, we were living our lives for ourselves and it felt good for the most part.

My breathing was hardened by now, fully regaining consciousness, I noticed Temi fixated on my crouch, my morning wood seemed to have gotten her attention and when she realized that I was looking at her, I could see the embarrassment in her eyes, she immediately turned her face to the ground in shear awkwardness as I reached for my inhaler and relieved myself.

Temi had always been the girl I thought was pretty but never had the intention of doing anything with, she was the girl who at the beginning of my friendship with Tola had been the annoying little sister who picked on her brother's friends. To her, I was ugly and could never be beautiful enough, but as we grew older and began to develop, the teasing reduced and she became one of the boys.

But everything changed when we all went for an overnight cinema, someone had thought up the idea to show movies overnight at a lower rate for young and struggling adults, Tola had invited his girlfriend Oluchi, and Temi because I had complained about him bringing his girlfriend to all our hangouts, they were in the honeymoon phase of their relationship and had no respect for single me, they were always kissing and fooling around, leaving me to stare at the ceiling. I figured I was done being in such awkward situation, I hated being the third wheel, Oluchi and I never had anything to say to each other, and after much bugging from Tola to check out the overnight cinema together, I told him I wouldn't go out with him and Oluchi unless there was a fourth person.

"Guy I said I don't want to be the third wheel, I didn't say you should bring your sister to join me" I had said in protest to his sister tagging along "but misery loves company" he had said mockingly. That movie night ended up with Temi cuddling up on me while Tola and Oluchi did what ever rubbish, young horny couples did.

That day was very unsettling, it was the first time I saw Temi as a woman and not Tola's junior sister, I began to avoid her because after that day I began noticing her, I started noticing how the little drops of sweats on her nose whenever she is busy made her looked insanely beautiful, and how her eyes which looked like she is about to fall asleep made her look hypnotizing.

And because it felt wrong to have something with your best friend's sister except you want to marry her, I avoided her, she was still the girl who spent a whole year calling *iyama* (rubbish) because a teacher had tried to convince her to play Mary while I play Joseph in our junior secondary school Christmas play.

It was easy to distance myself from her because we exactly didn't have anything in common except for the occasional jabs and insults which sometimes we both enjoyed.

We lived in a two bedroom apartment, one room served as our living room during the day and my bedroom at night and sometimes Temi's when she is around. Tola and his girlfriend, Oluchi who practically lived with us took the other, Tola coarsed me into this arrangement by promising he and his girlfriend would take care of our feeding and I wouldn't need to go into the kitchen, I hated cooking and I wasn't very good at it, my mother made sure I had the basics on locks, rice, beans, stew, and according to her, she didn't give birth to a child who would turn his wife into a slave or a maid. Tola's deal felt fair and if ever I was to bring a girl home I could have their room, Oluchi had her own apartment which wasn't far from ours, but she is super clingy and has an irritating need for attention, she had reported me to Tola once, saying I don't like her, because of a party we all attended. In that party I had said she wasn't my type during a game of truth or dare, Tola had told me I hurt her feelings by saying that. I was so disgusted, I couldn't see why I had to rub her ego because she was fucking my friend.

This might not be useful, but I think you should know that Tola's mother isn't in the country, she chose career over family as opposed to the conservative lifestyle his father wanted for her. After their divorce, Tola's mother moved abroad leaving my friend and Temi with their father.

But unlike the days of our childhood, Temi and Tola have now become distant, and although they spent days together under the same roof, they barely said anything of substance to each other, their parents divorce caused a spilt in their relationship, there were now sides, Tola took his mother's while Temi took her father's. According to Tola their mother wasn't allowed to fulfil her full potentials and if their father hadn't made himself an obstacle on the road to her dreams they will still be a family. But as for Temi, their mother was selfish for abandoning them and for making her career more important than their well being. Temi cut off all contacts with their mother and despised Tola for still being in touch with her. they were more of cordial strangers than brother and sister, they talked less and rarely argued and because Temi was usually around in our house there was always some unspoken tension in the air.

Our apartment is part of a story building. We shared the top floor with a young family, I sometimes look at them and get reminded of what I don't want for my life, a family of 5, three children of which comprised of a set of twins not more than 3 years old and a baby not more than a year. The picture I saw of them anytime they were out was depressing, the mother looked exhausted, lean, holes around the neck bone, she was wasting away and was too tired to even bother. The father on the other hand had stress written all over his face, he was nonchalant about the jumping and screaming of his kids, he left his malnourished wife to deal with them, all the times I saw them he rarely gave her a glance talk less of talking to her.

The few times I saw the wife smile was when she was being teased by Tola, Tola has always felt the need to be cordial with everyone, he felt the need to be liked and this for some reason had a huge effect on the wife who everyone calls Iya Ibeji , it seemed she was living off Tola's words, she craved to be seen, to be noticed, Tola's teasing and mild flirting made her feel like a person, a small part of me started thinking she had a crush on him, and I couldn't blame her, for most days she was not a person but an extension of her husband and children, since we started living there, up to this point, I never heard someone say her name, she was always called Iya Ibeji (mother of twins),her identity lost between being a wife and a mother, so it didn't seem Ludacris for her to grow fund of Tola, someone who actually saw and noticed her, it was just saddening how much attention she craved and might never get.

There was a time she was on her way out, Tola called her to say she looked nice, she paused, looked at the ground with a huge smile on her face, and when she finally raised up her head, I saw a tear fall from her eyes and gracefully hit the ground.

The young family weren't the only characters that caught my attention in that compound, there was Iya Wande (Wande's mother) a middle aged woman who was always spitting, shouting and sometimes she would laugh to self, there were different stories going around about her, the one that really bothered me was the one claiming her husband abandoned her for a younger woman, people had said that the younger woman used black magic to steal her husband and also to make her mad.

This story hauntingly felt true because when she had one of what seemed to be her episodes, she would scream "e gbami yemisi fe gba oko mo mi lowo" (please help me, Yemisi wants to steal my husband).

Children were cautioned to avoid her and adults tried to limit their contact, there was this believe that madness could be transmitted through bites, people who were less superstitious stayed away from her because she smelled, she rarely took her baths and rarely attended to her hair, except from when she was visited by her daughter who was believed to be Wande the only child she had for the husband who abandoned her, Wande would oddly remind me of Yewande my UNI girlfriend, they had the same name and the same effect on me, my heart who literally leap when they walked into a room. I would spend a huge part of my day looking at her wondering about her life, what was it like, what was she like, but I never took time out to ask.

Many people tried to convince Wande to move in with her mother or get someone to, but all she did was smile and tell them she would think about it, Wande didn't talk much which made her hard to read, but Iya wande fascinated me, to be crazy with pride, I looked at her with envy and sometimes with gratitude, because I knew being free from judgement, to not be aware that people are even judging is something I really craved, I had no idea then that one day I would end up like her, but this is not what I expected it to be like, maybe it's because I am stuck here.

There was this particular time, she came out to the compound, one of the neighbors was cooking akara to share for the people around in honor of her dead father, but immediately Iya Wande was handed a few pieces of akara, she threw them on the ground and smiled at the woman who gave it to her. When she was confronted about it, she simply said her pastor told her it was sinful to eat food dedicated to the dead, and despite the condemnation of those around claiming she had done something insulting, she didn't seem to be bothered by their disapproval, she just kept smiling.

She had done in public what they all did in the privacy of their own homes, I found pieces of akara in the bin days after, this is one of the side effects of colonial religion, it has made us lose trust in ourselves and in the beliefs we were born in. It has also made us hypocrites because it was customary to share akara after the death of a person, but the pentecostal churches had now made it seem like anyone who partakes in anything mildly cultural must be either a witch or wizard.

I had an habit staying back to watch Iya Wande and anticipating what she will do next, I didn't want to go crazy, but I envied getting to that point of oblivion where judgment didn't matter.

I have always had this compulsive urge to walk bare foot in the rain, it was easy to do this as a child, but the picture of a 20 years old man walking bare foot in the rain, will make people start raising eye brows.

I don't know why I always have the urge to do this, I just love how the cold sips through the underneath of my feet, it is oddly soothing but I have to deny myself of this feeling as I denied myself of other things because I don't want to come off as odd, crazy or stupid.

I seem to have derailed from my story, I think it's best I get back to it. So, at the office later that day, things were peculiarly dull, not that there was ever anything of interest, but this dullness was so peculiar, even my co workers were suffering from it. This particular day I wasn't the only one with an earpiece drowning myself in an isolation of my making.

This was the point where I wasn't sure why I was working anymore, the pay was terrible, I was writing about topics I would never read and they weren't even original contents, I, a graduate of English, who professor Makanju during my finals wanted to withhold as a graduate assistant was now reduced to rewriting gossip news from other gossip blogs. My parents weren't on board with me taking Professor Makanju's offer, to them being in the educational system was you setting yourself up for a life of unpaid salaries and to them, was a waste of my potentials, I was irritated by my job, it was also a waste of my potentials and my parents knew it, but they will rather choke on their own vomit than admit professor Makanju's offer was far better.

My co workers gave me grieve for resenting my job causing my original isolation. According to them, I was a spoilt child who felt like a job should be more about fulfilment rather than making money, they would say " *shebi*, you just graduated, I give you a year, after Nigeria hits you blue black, you will be grateful for what you get, how many people do you think get a job immediately they graduate, its because you're lucky you're talking rubbish" , and despite my resentment for my work I didn't leave, because I was indeed lucky to get the job, there are a lot of people with big dreams that have failed chasing a life of fantasy instead settling and accepting their reality. I see their examples everyday, I was lucky to get a job that paid, and paid on time, a job that didn't owe salaries and I wasn't going to give that all up because I could do so much better, there exactly isn't anything in my life that showed I was special.

Anyways, That day everything changed for me was when I decided to post the link of an article I just finished writing on my personal blog on twitter. I think you should pay attention to this because this explains a lot about where you guys found me.

"*heyy*, I'm having troubles opening the link" she texted me, that text would be what would later on change everything. "okay I will check it out thanks" I quickly responded, and then went through her page looking for information about her. I still don't have an idea why I was curious, there wasn't anything compelling about her, I was just curious, and the only information I could come across was that she was pretty.

"try this", I sent her a new link

"hey I can access the website now, thank you" she responded after a while

"I love the way you write, you're an amazing writer"

"thank you, it means a lot"

"I am a huge fan" she said and accompanied with the shy monkey emoji.

"awwn thanks, let's continue talking on WhatsApp"

"okay cool, 08154326128".

Before her, I never had anything serious, during my days in the university, I was on and off with Yewande, she was more concerned about how people saw her and not exactly how they felt about her, she terrified me but I enjoyed our back and forth, once, she confronted me in the middle of school screaming "you, you., you, why have you been ignoring my calls?" she was neurotic when I ignored her but when we were together, she wouldn't be present, it felt like she needed my attention but didn't need me.

*

later, on my way home, I had to walk through and alley, I noticed a shadow which wasn't mine steady following me, I tried speeding up my pace but still was unable to get rid of this mystery person, scared to turn back to face what seemed to be imminent danger, I started jogging, my heart throbbing, my mind racing, I was brought out of my fear and into consciousness when I accidently bumped into somebody, that was when I looked back and saw the Ghanaian man, he was the one who had been following me and when we made eye contact, he turned and disappeared into the dark.

Chapter 2

Instead of going straight to work the next day, I headed to the ATM, I needed to always have enough money on me because in Lagos not having enough money can get you killed, about 3 years ago, my mother had gone to deliver a package to one of her church members, she had gone without cash or her ATM card, she claimed she forgot and immediately she highlighted at where she was told to highlight, she was ambushed by robbers, but after realizing that she had no money or ATM card on her, she was seriously beating, her bags taken and also the package she went to deliver.

She came home all bruised up and raining curses on the church member she was suppose to deliver the package to, she felt the whole incident was a set up, she didn't feel it was a coincidence that the robbers happen to be where she was told to highlight. My mother has never been the trusting type which was one of the reoccurring issues in her fights with my father, that was something being religious didn't change about her. It was just a surprise the robber did not leave with her car, *"omo ye ma ya werey Loru ko jesu"* (that girl will go insane in Jesus name), you see, where I come from, mental health and more specifically schizophrenia is the ultimate punishment for evil doing, there is nothing natural about mental health, there has to be spirits or curses behind it, which raises the question, am I here because of some curse or punishment for something I have done?

Money doesn't survive in Lagos, it leaves three times faster than how it comes in, there is a compulsion to spend when you are in Lagos and to make matters worse the cost of living is unreasonably high, I needed money management lessons and I knew it, my salary barely lasted a week and I could no longer afford falling under the Lagos spell if I was going to survive adulthood.

The queue at the ATM was almost none existent, there was just one person before me and after I made my withdrawal, and after, I heard words that shook me to my core, "let me see that thing in your hand". This is Lagos, a city once listed among the most dangerous in the world and even though it is a lot calmer compared it's glory days of daylight robberies and people getting burnt alive with car tires, the shadows of the past still lurked around.

I immediately put my card and money in my pocket which made the only thing in my hand at the time a Sidney Sheldon book, 'Windmill of the gods'.

I handed the book over to the man who those words came out from. I expected it to be returned to me after a quick glance but that wasn't the case, he clenched to my book and said " I am a police man" and in that moment I knew my safety was hanging in the balance, the number one threat to Nigerians, isn't the robbers, it isn't Boko haram or the kidnappers, the number threat to Nigerians is the police, and in that moment I was taken back to my last encounter with a policeman.

I was disoriented in computer village, the place which harbors the largest number of laptops, computers and phones accessories in Nigeria and I am willing to bet the whole Africa, when I was much younger I thought the name computer village was given to this place because computers came alive and lived there. It is a place where people get robbed and get cheated. It is a tough place to be, people come out crying, people lose money, it is where the phone I had wanted to fix got stolen by the person I had paid to fix it. The thief approached me claiming to be a phone technician, he took me to a small shop which sold phones and phone accessories, he fiddled with the phone for sometime, opening it up, loosing bolts and screwing them back in, he convinced me he needed to get something, I followed him knowing fully well you can't trust anyone in computer village, we had heard stories of people being sold cardboards thinking they purchased television set, only to come to the realization of their misfortune when they got home.

My senses failed me that day, because I had no idea when I handed him all the money with me until I lost sight of him, there were stories about the people who operate in computer village, it was said that some of the thieves use black magic to wash their faces so as to scan out suitable target for their diabolical acts, this black magic was said to make people zone out and not realize they were being robbed until the act was done and the thieves were long gone.

18 There is nothing romantic about death

Now in the middle of computer village, disoriented with the reality of everything, the reality of losing my phone, I went back to the shop I was taken to to ask about the thief and if they could help me trace him, they denied knowing and laughed while doing it, one of them even claimed they didn't see me with any guy, another said he thought the thief was my brother. Looking and feeling very stupid, I decided to buy what we Nigerians call a China phone, these were poorly assembled phones which were imported from China, the kind of phone which had Samsung branded on the case but showed techno once you switched it on.

That day wasn't just mine because that was when police man accosted me, he put his hand on my shoulder and said " I am a police officer, what is inside your bag"

trying to keep my composure, I replied, "it my laptop"

"where is the receipt"

"its not with me"

"so you stole it"

This was how every young Nigerian was robbed, killed or jailed by the Nigerian police force, not being able to provide the receipt of what ever was on you made the police immediately assumed you stole it. I don't know if they believe people who walk around without receipts stole everything on them or they just use the fact that a person is without receipts to extort and harass harmless individuals.

"I can show you my laptop, there is proof that I am the owner, I have my pictures and my documents in it"

"I don't need to see anything, show me your ID card"

I brought out my then school ID card and handed it over to him, he inspected it and handed it back to me

"are you sure its only the laptop that is in your bag?"

"yes sir" I said with fear and cooperation mixed in my mouth.

"I am taking you to the station, you will have to bail yourself"

The news about the corruption of the Nigerian police system wasn't new to me but this was my first time encountering it, people have spent years doubting their training, some even went has far as probing their mental capacity. I knew this could be the end of me if I didn't give him the money he was going to ask me, he was about to take me to the police station when I hadn't committed a crime and I wasn't even accused of committing one, he also was going to make me pay to bail myself when according to authorities bail is supposed to be free.

The justice system of the country is a death trap, people who are taken to the station hardly get out, there are people who have been locked up for over a decade and have never faced trial, so when he told me he was taking me to the station, my whole life flashed before my eyes.

"or do you have money now, so you just bail yourself before we get to the station, because if you get to the station, it might take a while before you get out" he continued drawing me out of my thoughts

" ha please sir, I just got robbed, I don't have any money on me"

so you want me to take you to the station?"

After going back and forth between plea and threats, I succumbed and surrendered 5 thousand naira to him,

I know my stories have stories in them, you will just have to forgive me, this is the only way I can tell it.

At the ATM stand I was now faced with what I thought was a similar situation and I tried to convince myself that I was smarter and wiser, I wasn't going to let this one trap me like that, I was going to excuse myself as quick as I can

"I like people that read, I appreciate them" confused and perplexed I struggled to show a smile

"you know what, come and sit down and wait for me" he gestured towards the bench that was placed for people willing to use the ATM

"my name is inspector Shedrack, I like people that read, let me give you my number I'll introduce you to my library" I had never faced a situation like this before, a police man that doesn't want to collect anything from me instead wants to give me something, my instincts weren't okay.

He handed me a small piece of paper and a pen "take, write my number down, you can call me anytime, I will introduce you to my library."

"thank you sir"

"see I am a useless man, but I am a good policeman, I have been drinking since 6 am but have I insulted you?"

"no" I replied confused as to why I just got that information

"come let me take you to a bar, I will buy you malt so we can talk"

Not understanding what was going on, I protested, "sir I am already late for work.."

"okay, let me follow you to where you will take maruwa"

Thankfully the *maruwa* stand was just a five steps walking distance away from the ATM, and before I could board one of the yellow tricycles, the Ghanaian came out of no were, this was the second time I was seeing him, since our first meeting.

He forcefully held my hand and in my struggle to free myself, he said "we are not going to chase you anymore, you are going to come to us" and immediately, he walked away.

"you are going to come to us" the voice of the policeman almost made me jump out of my skin, his eyes were hallow and his voice grave and after saying his cryptic message, he staggered away, like a zombie.

~

A week after all the awkwardness, everything went back to normal, Temi and I went back to throwing subliminal shades at each other, Tola and Oluchi still couldn't get their hands off each other and it felt like things were finally right with the world. But I couldn't help all the superstitious beliefs from creeping in. They kept saying "you will come to us" the police man and the crazy Ghanaian. There have been stories of people being kidnapped and being used for money rituals, every other day there is news about the police apprehending a ritualist with human body parts, this was something I should tell my parents but I figured nights of fasting and prayers were going to be the last resort and since I haven't been physically threatened by these people, there was no need to subject myself to biblical torture and giving my parents one more thing to hold over me, I just wished for them to be some sort of bad dream.

There were days my superstition really shock me and during those days I almost called my Aunty Kemi, she is well vast in superstitious and strange things, she had carried her infant child to a native doctor because she felt he could stop him from dying, after two back to back still births she was convinced her child was an *'abiku'* a spirit child who came to the world to die, and when a child like that comes to the world, they are marked by making an incision on their body preferably the face, some people even go as far as cutting off a toe or finger, while some burn the child so they can recognize the child incase he decides to come back to life, all this was done so as to prevent the parents from getting attached to a child who was eventually going to die.

After my cousin was scarred , he decided to stay alive, according to my aunt he realized he had been caught and would be noticed if he dies and decides to come back to life.

I was never a fan of superstition but the thing with the Ghanaian was really troubling and to get my mind off everything, I started chatting with the girl from twitter and it felt good, I didn't feel this way even with Yewande, I still find my relationship with Yewande a bit troubling, it seemed like my staying with her was because some where deep inside me I felt nobody else was going to have sex with me, and I was grateful to her because she did, I ignored all her flaws because she was sleeping with me. Apart from the adrenaline that only fueled irrationality, what I had with Yewande was intense and brief, there was nothing about our time together that left a lasting memory, apart from energetic efforts towards pleasing our heightened libido.

This was not exactly how my relationship with Yewande started, in the beginning we bonded over scarred pasts and weird interests, for example our hamburger hunt, this adventure was inspired by the SpongeBob character and his krabby paddies, in mainland Lagos there were only few places that sold real hamburgers on our then budget, the ones near by, most of the eateries Yewande and I visited either had, only meat between the breads, no lettuce, no cheese, nothing, and in some places there wasn't even any meat but in those places there was lettuce, if you could call it that.

22   There is nothing romantic about death

When we finally found a place in Ikeja city mall which sold the real deal, we both confused that moment for love, it was the first time and the only time we said the L word to each other, our love for food and also the love to hunt it down, made me lose my virginity. I shared this same interest and love for food with the new twitter girl whose name is Morenike.

Morenike was petite and had facial similarities with the sun emoji, this made her look adorable, but when it came to appearance, she wasn't typically my type, like every other ignorant hormonal young adult, I too subscribed to popular media's definition of sexy, big bum, big boobs and tiny waist, but there was something about Morenike which made her intriguing, she always had stories to tell and this took me back to the times when my care was left in the hands of house helps, when my parents were too busy and troubled to take care of me and I was too young to take cafe of myself.

There was this particular help who we called Aunty Blessing, before bed time I would coil up beside her and listen to her tell stories, one the stories she told which never left me was the story of two brothers, they went on a great adventure to decide which of them would be the king, they were asked by the village chiefs to go into the forest and procure the most beautiful flower, whoever comes back with the most beautiful flower ends up becoming the king.

The older brother scared of the competition killed his younger brother in the forest when he found out his younger brother's flower was prettier than the one he got. years later and after the elder brother had pretended not to know about his brother's demise and had intensely mourned him, he was made king. A hunter from the village went hunting and stumbled on the bones of the dead younger brother which had now become a flute. I felt the story a little unrealistic, but my childhood brain did not bother to probe the unrealistic nature of the story, I was more intrigued by the bone singing flute when the hunter blew it, the voice of the younger brother came out singing " hunter hunter, that is my bone you're blowing, my brother killed me inside forest, he took away all my flower, because he wants to be a king, hunter hunter , that is my bone you are blowing, hunter, hunter".

I had a huge crush on Aunty Blessing and this was because of the singular fact that she was able to transport me to another world with the stories and words that came out her mouth, when she left us, I remember crying, but the strange thing is the more I grew the more I forgot what she looked like which then made me idolize her the more.

Morenike in some way reminded me of Aunty Blessing, the help that shook my family's foundation to the core, and in some way she seemed like someone who like Aunty Blessing was destined to go away.

Morenike had a wild imagination and a huge sense of humor, during one of our WhatsApp conversations before our first meeting, she had told me, she had no belly button, I had protested that it wasn't possible,

"I have a rare birth defect," she had simply said, and when I asked for a picture of her belly,

"you will just have to see me" was all she said in response

On our first meeting Morenike and I were sitting side by side, our bodies nearly entering each other, our minds bursting with things we would do together and to each other, but first we had to say something, break the ice, play our part and role in the universal human mating ritual.

"let me see your belly button" I said with an aura of uncertainty.

"*ehn?*" she replied and busted into laughter

Then she did something, which looking back at now was something so basic but for some reason I still don't understand was the singular act that made me fall in love with her. She rolled up her shirt and showed me her belly button

"well are you satisfied? I'm sure you are relieved to know that I am not a test tube baby"

at that point I couldn't stop smiling.

" I am not Kyle XY" she said with a flirtatious smile, Kyle XY was this TV series we (I'm guessing everyone in my age bracket) watched when we were young, it's about a boy who was grown in a government lab and lacked a belly button because he didn't develop in the womb and so didn't need an umbilical cord which meant no belly button.

"but you know Kyle XY was trash" I said

"what?!" she said with a poor attempt to sound alarmed

"its true, everything is just stupid, I can't believe I enjoyed it as a kid"

"I cant believed this" she said smiling "I can't believe I am attracted to a guy who thinks Kyle XY is trash"

I was silent for a while, and tried to take the moment in, it was a moment I wanted to remember so I had to make sure I captured everything,

"when was the last time you watched it?" I asked her

I think I was in JSS 3 or SS 1"

" this is why you think it is good, I used to think so too until I watched it recently, it is because you watched the series when you had no care in the world, life was easy, you had baby crushes and you were receiving love notes, so when you remember Kyle XY you associate it with those feelings, but if you watch it now that life is hard, you will hate it as much as I do or even more"

she laughed uncontrollably for a while and then said " wait first, who told you life is hard for me?"

" life is hard for everyone living in Nigeria"

she paused and just looked at me for a while and said " you are funny and really smart too"

Then, there was silence between us again, this was a different kind of silence, it was void of awkwardness and for the first time in my life, I felt like I was in a kiss scene from an Hollywood romantic movie, I could feel the slow motions and the leaning in, I could also feel the mellow music playing in the background except from the middle age people who were around us and I couldn't help but wonder if since my absence of participation in the human mating rituals, Nigeria has evolved, less judgmental and public display of affection was now allowed. Too scared to find out I fondled my way to find her belly button and she laughed and said "what are you doing?"

"I'm trying to make sure your belly button is still there"

she busted into an array of laughter later that night during our late night call, I said " I should have kissed you" and with that mellow voice of hers which will later be music to me, she said "of course you should have"

"maybe next time then," I said

"yeah, maybe next time".

Chapter 3

Love is drug, and just like every other substance addiction, it slowly creeps in, then sucks you in and then encompasses you, it takes over your day and then takes over your night, you can't imagine your day without it, you develop panic attacks and withdrawal symptoms if it stays too long away from you.

This was exactly what happened with Morenike and I. We didn't meet for a while after our first meeting, but it felt like we talked every minute in-between. I was scared of seeing her, scared of the way I was falling, scared of the vulnerability I was developing, I was scared because of how hard it was going to be when she finally decides to leave.

We talked about heavy things, we talked about the death of her family, this made me realize I am attracted to broken people, people with tragedy. I remember noticing Yewande and getting close to her after her uncle caused a scene in school because her grades were dropping and according to him she making sure her parents death were in vain, it was a huge scandal back in UNI, it was even said that she tried to kill herself after that incident, I never spoke to her about it, I just developed and interest which led to 2 years of blissful toxicity. I don't know if it was Morenike's hatred of society or the tragedy that surrounded her that kept drawing me in.

Like most things in my country, nothing is ever done well, and Moreinke's family was just another casualty of the Nigerian system as a whole, It was supposed to be another boring night in Morenike's household but a dangerous volt of energy went into their house and sparked the tiny fridge in her father's room. Morenike was lucky not to be in the house that night, her mother had sent her to a friend's place to get a wedding attire *(aso ebi)*. She came back to see her house up in flames and an audience of people in the streets, it took a while for people to realize she wasn't in the house, they expected her to be roasting in the burning flames, her family was very reserved and no one was expected to be out especially at that time of the night, but her mother had been overwhelmed at home preparing for a wedding that was supposed to happen the next day, which was why she had to send Morenike to go get the *aso ebi*, something she normally wouldn't do.

In the years to come, Morenike would think of that day with so much significance, when talking about it she would say " I didn't only escape death, I escaped a life".

Morenike's parent were overly religious, they belonged to a church which banned television and every form of circular entertainment. According to their pastor, television was one of the avenues the devil uses to communicate with the world, at home, the morning devotion was 4 hours, they always got to school by 10AM and on a bad day 12PM which was after recess, her parents excuse was that they had no power except that of God's, Her and brother were flogged at school until their teachers got tired, and became passively aggressive towards them, they made sure Morenike and her brother were discriminated against and were treated less than their peers, they felt Morenike and her brother came late because they felt above the law. The owner of the school was a close family friend who always interceded for them anytime they were to face punishments.

Their parents didn't do anything about this, they didn't even go to the school to intervene on behalf of their kids, her father would always say "I have no other power than the power of God". they were always chased by enemies, her parents were in constant paranoia, they were constantly in church, they were constantly fasting, doing vigils and in prayer meetings. When she told me this, she told me with immense guilt because to her it didn't feel right to feel relieved by the death of her family, she did love them, but she resented how life would have been if they were still around. The week before her family's demise her parents made Morenike and her younger brother go through a seven week marathon vigil. the vigil spanned through out 5 school days because her mother recently lost her job and her father had also failed at yet another business attempt and they felt there was something supernatural about their failures. Both her and her little brother were not allowed to sleep during the vigil until it came to an end by 4am, and because their bodies weren't machines, the first day of the vigil they went to bed by 4am and got up around 10am. They decided they weren't going to go to school because of how late they were, but their parents weren't having it, they made sure they went after their 4 hours morning prayers, because none of their children were going to stay at home when school was going on.

Their parents had demons, both parents were products of polygamous households, and as it was the custom of churches like theirs, they were made to believe that there were spiritual battles over their destinies and progress, Morenike's father had failed at several businesses and her mother, was refused several promotion and benefits at her work place before eventually being fired, her parents were always waking up with one nightmare or the other, plagued by things they had done in their past.

That day, they couldn't go to school because they felt their presence was going to be an insult to the institution, they got out of the house by 2pm and wandered aimlessly around town for two hours, they made sure to avoid routes their parents took and also made sure they didn't treed places where people close to their parents or the school would notice, they made sure that incident never happened during the remainder of the week long vigil. they made sure they didn't go to sleep after the vigil, they bought coffee and instead of making it with milk or drinking it black, they poured it raw in their mouths whenever they started dozing.

They still got to school late, they were still made fun of, but no one knew what they had to do to make sure they got to school at that time they did.

She said I was the only one she told this, people expected her to idolize her parents, she loved them and was hurt by their death, but she loved the life she had with her uncle, her father's brother more. He was a Christian but not a fanatic, she went early to school, she didn't pray as much, she didn't exactly believe in God because despite how much her parents were involved in their religion they ended up dying in the worst possible way. Her baby brother was also caught in that fire, he was the one she idolized. On his birthdays, she would take a long walk and get herself two cheap ice-creams, it reminded her of their time together, it reminded her of the day they aimlessly wandered because they were too embarrassed to go to school, the day their parents forced them to get to school at 2pm. It's been 10 years since the demise of her family, there were times when she forgot about her brother's birthday during the early period after their death, those times when ever she remembered, she would cry herself to sleep, now she says she sometimes struggle to remember what her brother looks or sounds like, she carries the guilt and sadness around, sometimes she questions her life, what exactly did she do to deserve life over the rest of her family?

*

Morenike now became a routine, she was who I texted first in the morning and the last person I texted at night. She expected me to take things to the next level, it's been a month since our first physical meeting and I had not asked her out yet, I hadn't even told Tola about her and this was mainly because of Temi, she always had a way of making me feel bad about things I was excited about.

I also hadn't kissed Morenike, every time we met, we shook hands and our hugs always lingered, we say 'bye' for about 10 times before actually leaving. I haven't felt like this with anyone, my anxiety was getting the best of me, I began to think maybe I wasn't good enough, and I might fuck everything up with a kiss.

I had deep rooted insecurities surrounding intimacy, Yewande left me with a kiss. After a nice pizza date, she held me in the middle of the road, tiptoed and kissed me for about 11 seconds, I was never really comfortable with public display of affection because in Lagos Nigeria, people hardly minded their business, they are also annoyingly self righteous, in the heat of our expression of love, with our lips locked, a woman walked up to us with disapproval written all over her face, according to her what we were doing was against God, and we lacked home training, we just smiled and continued sticking our tongues down each other's throats.

I dreaded confrontation, but for her I was willing to commit social suicide, after the self righteous woman left us, she looked me in the eyes and said, "please don't cheat on me" I gave her words of affirmation just to put her mind at rest. Later that night, at a friend's party which I took her to, she cheated on me with my friend while I was still at the party and the worst part was they had the sex in public, another friend had discovered them at a corner and brought the attention of the entire party.

Nobody saw or heard from her after that day, but when I finally got a hold of her, she told me she already had another boyfriend "I just needed someone mature" was all she could say and after months of self torture, going through her socials, seeing her happy with another guy, I deleted her number and blocked her off all my socials, and even though I had her out of my life, the scars she left behind still runs deep.

Rumors circulated around at that period that she cheated and left because I was not particularly good in bed, Yewande never really explained why she left, how she went from begging me not to break her heart to shattering mine in less than 24 hours, for several months I had nightmares about her and her new boyfriend being intimate and making fun of me .

And now that I was with Morenike, I was terrified of going for a kiss talk less of being intimate, the dark clouds of inadequacy followed me around and it was beginning to seem like she was going to leave me for it, I wanted to kiss her, I desperately did, but anytime I was about to, I was overcome by this crippling anxiety. I used to be eager for intimacy, my first experience with Yewande, She was already experience, so the discovery was mostly on my part, I got initialed in the sweet sweet pleasure and euphoric feeling of having a female take control of my genitals, it was one of those cliché UNI chronicles, boy has an apartment outside the school, girl comes over from time to time and they chill out, this particular evening, she brought alcoholic energy drinks after our hamburger adventure, we both drank and drank, everything quickly went from poorly singing along to a song to her unzipping my trousers, the music continued playing but the room got hotter, and everything seem to be at a stand still except us and the music. After doing things we were told to stay away from until marriage, we laughed and did it some more.

But now that memory seemed like it was from someone's else's life, I couldn't even kiss the girl I was beginning to fall in love with.

In one of our last meetings, I met Morenike at a little restaurant which was located towards the main road, it was positioned in such a way that people driving could see. She came with her cousin, who was also pretty and petite but not as pretty as Morenike. We sat for a while, the attendant came to take our order , I looked at Morenike's cousin and said "*shey* you see this girl beside you *ehn*, I am going to marry her" everyone around the table started blushing even the restaurant attendant who had no business in what we were saying was smiling sheepishly

"you want to marry me *abi*, hope you are ready to pay my *bride price*" Morenike said with a smug on her face

"why will I pay bride price when it's not slave trade"

"it's just tradition, customary, it symbolizes that you value me"

"and my value should be in the way I treat you not by spending money, you are not a property, that's one of the things that enables domestic violence and the demeaning of women."

"that doesn't make any sense"

I laughed, smiled at her and said "anyways when are you leaving for school?"

Morenike was a student of the university of Ibadan which according to the Nigerian map, if I should have acted on how I felt I would have ended in a long distance relationship, our getting to know each other happened when she was still in Lagos and I got to know about her UNI when I had already fallen

"next week" she said in a way that made me feel like she was reminding me that I had to do something before she leaves.

I smiled as we enjoyed our meal, the evening was good, too good, her cousin gave us space to talk as we were leaving, she rushed to the front, and when it came to where we were supposed to part ways I could feel my heart literally sinking

"okay, so see you later" I said as I drew her into my arm secretly praying that we dissolved into each other

"yeah bye" she said as she pulled away but still holding my hands, and her eyes screaming at me to do something, I could hear them loud and clear, but before I could overcome my unnecessary fear, I saw the Ghanaian man, who screamed "you will come to us!" and this time I had my mild blackout.

Chapter 4

Nothing good last forever, and it was silly of me to think that this would have ended up differently, when it comes to me, things end before they even begin. Work was beginning to get to me, the picture of my life was becoming more glaring, I was beginning to fall into my parent's reality, a reality filled with overwhelming dissatisfaction.

My boss had decided that I wasn't going to earn as much as my colleagues because I hadn't done my youth service which to me was total unfair, nothing about this was talked about when I was taking the job, and I was allocated the same responsibilities as my colleagues.

The youth service program was created after the civil war, young people were shipped to places away from their state of origin to serve and learn about other communities.

This made sense on paper, to prevent another civil war, the best thing was to have everyone get a first hand experience of each other's culture and way of life, but like everything in Nigeria, over the years, it's wasn't well sustained. now, youth service feels like losing a year, there is nothing you gain in the whole experience that helps set you up for the life you have ahead. Nigeria is hard, you are shipped to another state, to serve a rural community as a school teacher for a year, a year you could have used being productive and building your résumé, gain some experience to better yourself . I know this might sound selfish, but again Nigeria is hard, the government has done nothing to assist the young people, the security in the country is shit and the youth service is just another avenue to put your life at risk especially when you get posted to the North. Most people go as far as bribing their way into getting posted to the south, west or east where they might get business opportunities but most importantly where they wouldn't get killed.

I was still going to do this youth service thing because of events like what was happening at my office, it wasn't just my time yet, I was being deprived because I had not yet wasted a year of my life, didn't feel fair but there was nothing I could do about it.

To be honest, I don't only hate my Job, I hate my career part, my parents had hated the idea of me studying creative arts, they called it a waste of time, they wanted me to do something more related to science or business because that was were the world was headed, they settled for English because according to them, everything is better than the arts.

I am a good writer, but I hate writing, my true passion is visual artistry, but there isn't a structure for creatives in Nigeria and I had no idea where to start from, the only future I could see for myself was to be a starving road artist, who spends his life drawing politicians and musicians at the road side.

I tried building an online portfolio, but all I ever got was "this is beautiful" and nothing more, I never made any money from my drawings and this made it more difficult to quit this god forsaken job and I am not one of those people who blindly chase a dream without any clear cut plan because like I said there is nothing special about me.

I had sleepless nights about how I could get myself from where I am to an artist in the European galleries, but I couldn't see any clear journey, I had no artist friends, I had no artist mentors, I was alone in this journey and I was lost.

Work was shit and so was love, after the night out with Morenike and her cousin, I started having this sinking feeling, the feeling that told me everything wasn't going to be the same again, the feeling that told me everything was going to be down right bad, the feeling I had every time I see my parents together.

There was this particular night, the first time I felt my heart drown, I think I was about 12, my mother, just like all African mothers was on the phone with my dad's sister, the one who had stood by her during my delivery and when I developed my health crisis, she felt indebted to her and for some reason made it her job to make sure I was close to both this woman and her family, It wasn't like I had any problem with my aunt, I just always felt awkward on the phone, except from saying stuffs like "I'm fine ma" "thank you ma" "Amen ma" there was nothing else that came out of my mouth, her children were people I hadn't seen in my life, anytime we were on the phone, there was always this long pause before someone asks "what class are you now?".

My Aunt who was now out of the country called and my mother handed me the phone to talk to my cousin, I was reluctant in taking the call because my cousin had now developed an accent and I didn't just feel like saying "*ehn* what did you say?" my mom irritated by my hesitation, pulled me aggressively to her and scolded me after the 3 second conversation which was just filled with hi and hellos and also what class are you? questions.

She went on about how my aunt was the reason I am alive *blah, blah, blah*, my dad interrupted and accused her of trying to push me on his sister, it turned into an argument, the argument then got physical after my mother said "I wouldn't be trying to push him on your sister if you had been there for us when you got me pregnant and not chicken out like a coward".

Whenever I remember that moment, everywhere becomes dark and images of my dad hitting my mom continuously flashes through my mind, the neighbors had to come in, the elderly ones were talking to my parents while the young adults tried to keep me entertained. I could see it in their eyes they wished I didn't have to go through that, Aunty Blessing who recently moved back to our neighborhood after getting married to one of the neighbor's driver came to our house that night. She wrapped herself around me like a blanket, the warmth of her body made me forget about my parents, she pulled me away to her cramped self contain room apartment, , she made me sit on her lap, rested my head on her bosom, caressed my head, then she moved to my trousers, I didn't object, no words were said, she just smiled and continued what she was doing till the night faded into dark and the morning met me on my mother's bed.

My escapade with Aunty Blessing continued, after the first time, I always found myself going back, urging her to do what she did the last time, this continued for a while, until the nosey gateman, who was serving the same house as her husband badged in on us one afternoon after school, I felt that feeling, the feeling that my heart was sinking within me before a mini hell broke loose.

My parents decided to be parents, for the first time they were in agreement, they threatened Aunty blessing they were going to get her arrested, I didn't understand what was going on that day, why was everyone overreacting? I knew sex and anything related to it was shameful, but Aunty blessing didn't do a thing to me that I didn't want her to do and I was just as guilty and responsible as her.

My parents allegiance didn't last long as they began to blame each other, calling each other names, trying to making the other feel like they were the reason for my violation, after that night, what was left of our family was nothing more than cordiality, they didn't even try to fight anymore, there wasn't love and my parent wouldn't get a divorce because of God, they didn't want to be the one to be seen as the one who gave up on the marriage, so they pushed each other towards calling it off.

All these started with a feeling, a feeling of imminent doom, the feeling that I was about to lose everything and the feeling that I was about to self destruct. I have been having this since the last time I spoke to Morenike, something was about to go wrong and it was a matter of time, I knew it deep in my gut.

A week after our eatery meeting, Morenike's number wasn't reachable, and I didn't get a call or a message that showed she was alive, she had just moved to school, she was in her third year studying English but unlike me, she loved it. Radio silence from Morenike wasn't my only problem, Tola, Oluchi and Temi had found out about her, and they wouldn't shut up about it, Oluchi who finds a way to make everything about herself, kept insinuating that I kept whatever it was I had with Morenike from them because I didn't want her to get involved and start planning double dates. Temi resumed being the torn of my flesh saying things like "so someone can love this one *wawu*" "if Wole can find love then there is hope for everyone".

When I couldn't take it anymore, I told them I couldn't even get a hold of Morenike and they were getting excited over nothing.

"I just knew it, why will girl love this one" Temi said sarcastically

This radio silence from Morenike triggered my insecurities, Yewande too went silent on me when everything ended, it was beginning to feel like I was easily disposable.

There are moments in life where your heart will sink into a deep abyss, and you will be up most night struggling to get rid of this sinking feeling, hoping your heart will somehow find its way to the top of the sea of emotions and stay afloat.

This is what it felt like when Morenike finally called me, the call felt like she was doing it out of courtesy, according to her, she had been doing a lot of thinking and as if telling me she had feelings for me was to serve as some form of consolation, she went on to say, she couldn't do a long distant thing, she couldn't see how exactly it was going to work out for either of us, so she concluded it was best we end things before it got any serious.

*

Denial, one of the stages of grief, where you aren't ready to face reality so you bury yourself in an alternate universe where things are easier to swallow. This was where I was after my call with Morenike, we weren't in a relationship and I quite didn't want us to breakup before we got the chance to become something more. I began to spiral, what could have happened that would have caused her change of heart, was it because I didn't kiss her? I was being too slow, did she think I wasn't man enough? did she even like me? was Yewande right all along?

Tola had decided that we were going to take the day off to sulk and then get back to our lives. we have always been like this, anytime either of us was hurting we would take the day off, because, pain demanded to be felt and it won't go away until given full attention.

We learnt this after watching 'fault in our stars' it should have been four of us taking the day off to sulk, but the others were out of the country for masters and adulthood slaps you with unnecessary responsibility and sometimes it gets hard to breathe, keeping in touch sometimes feels like a luxury.

When I got my first heartbreak, the Yewande heartbreak, my friends traveled from their respective schools to get cramped up in Tola's architecture class, I was in the university of Lagos and Bisola the girl of our group wouldn't be able to be physically there for me if I had stayed in my school because of this dumb rule of not allowing girls into male hostels, maybe it wasn't dump, because Nigerian parents had failed to teach their boys how to treat women, the hostel which housed about 500 hundred boys had a culture of slut shaming and cat calling girls that walked pass the hostel, it was always unsettling and during the Yewande heartbreak I wasn't in the right frame of mind to deal with all of that.

We resulted to Tola's architecture class in Yabatech, slept on the hard wooden tables while we laughed, ate and all round tried to make me fill better, we enjoyed silence that night which I think strengthened our bond and help me survive the Yewande heartbreak.

I wasn't quite sure how much I had fallen for Morenike until our last conversation which left me with an emotion that I couldn't quite explain, I was hurt but I didn't feel I had the right to be, I hadn't know her enough and there wasn't any expressed commitment to feel that something was done to me.

Tola thought my situation was enough reason to get drunk, it was his recipe for dealing with pain, getting stupid drunk and waking up with an headache, he would say "when you get to the bottom of the bottle, you realize that what doesn't kill you shouldn't stop you from living your life" but instead of my four friend's this time, I had just Tola and his sister, Temi, who was at this time a drunkard in training to get me through the sulking.

Temi had her own reason to sulk, her mother was back in town for a few weeks, she had been made by her father to go visit. Their mother by some means we don't still understand found out about Temi's 33 years old boyfriend and was giving them grieve about the age gap "she is going to make Michael leave me" Temi said as she took her second shot of vodka, her mother had threatened Michael, she had told him if she ever caught him with her daughter again, he was going to sleep in prison, she had caused a big scene in public calling him a pedophile, Temi was 18 at this time and her father was okay with it, as the first daughter of the family he expected her to have trapped a man and start thinking of starting a family. " who does my mother think she is? how can she just come here an act like she cares after abandoning us for all those years" she said as she struggled to get back the cup of vodka I had just taken from her,

"I think that's enough drinking for you" I said

"I am not even drunk" she protested

I hadn't seen Temi this vulnerable before, she was yarning for her mother's love but was too stubborn to accept or admit it,

"where is Tola?" I asked watching Temi snatched her cup back from me

"he is on the phone with Oluchi"

"how do you know it's Oluchi?"

"who else calls him on his phone?" she said with a smirk on her face

"I am going to Oluchi's house, her roommates are out and you know she can't stay alone" Tola said as he hurried in to he pack some change over clothes

"why can't she come here?" Temi asked

"she said she is giving Wole space"

"*ha* Wole what did you do to her *oo*" Temi said giggling

"don't mind that drama queen" I said as I took a gulp of vodka

This is not the first time Tola had gone to stay with his girlfriend when her people were away, she was 21 and still scared of being alone, there is this story about the day her parents left her at home and went to a church vigil, she had just gotten home from school and had gone to bed immediately having no idea when her parents left for church.

When she woke up around 2.A.M, she looked for her parents and when she couldn't find them she called her father and asked him to come pick her from home, the poor man had to drive back home in the middle of the night just to take her to the vigil.

"so you are leaving me" I said watching him get ready to go out of the door

"guy she needs me" he said standing at the door waiting for my permission to leave, not that he needed it, but god forbid we made each other feel abandoned

"*no p sha*, be going, but I'm thinking of visiting Morenike in her school"

"*eh eh*, why do you want to do that?"

"I don't know, I just don't want to give up like that" I said as I gulped down my drink

" okay *sha*, so when you want to go?" "I don't know yet"

"okay"

"alright, kiss Oluchi good night for me. and don't forget to check for monsters under the bed" "you're mad" he laughed and walked out.

I tried standing up and it was a bit of a struggle, as it was seeming quite hard to find my balance, I collapsed on the ground, Temi laughed and joined me on the floor

"you are already drunk" she said

"no *jare*, I am just tipsy, I'll sleep it off now" I said while closing my eyes, Temi pulled me up to a sitting position, "I don't want you to sleep" she said, pushing our cups far from us and moving too close for comfort

I closed my eyes and heard her say "what do you want to do?"

"*err* I want to sleep?"

she pulled me close and traced her hand around my face, "I mean, what do you want to do with or on me?"

I was a bit startled by what she was saying, but somehow I found her proposition endearing and before I could hold myself, the words came rolling out of my mouth "I want to kiss you" This was a far cry from the relationship we had about a week ago, the hostility we shared had somehow metamorphosed into an intense sexual tension. And before I knew it, I was struggling with unhooking her bra. She broke off from me, pushed me, making sure I was lying flat and whispered in my ear, "let me take care of you", she pulled down trousers and proceeded into giving a blowjob but before I could ease into enjoying the pleasure, she vomited all over.

Chapter 5

What happened between Temi and I was followed by troubling emotions, firstly, I felt like I had stabbed my friend at the back, you don't do shit with your friend's sister, it was borderline incest, and there was also the part about her being intoxicated, I mean, I wouldn't take advantage of someone but after that night I didn't know anymore, a drunk or tipsy person can't give consent right? but I didn't have sex with her and I don't know if I eventually would have if she hadn't vomited. but I was tipsy too, I didn't plan to do anything, I wanted to sleep, she was the one who came to me, and started robbing my face, does that mean she raped me? or assaulted me? I don't know, sometimes I get the terms mixed up.

I couldn't face her after that night, I began avoiding her like a plague again, I decided I had to visit Morenike the next week, and guilt was eating me up, I couldn't bring myself to kiss Morenike, a girl who my heart leaped for but I could stick my dick in the mouth of Temi, a girl who has spent her entire existence making my life miserable.

Tola decided to tag along, and we headed for Ibadan which I sometimes mistake for Ife, one of them was the home of the Yorubas, my dad would tell me stories about Oduduwa, he would also narrate the link the Yorubas had with the people of Benin, I never paid attention to those stories, because all his stories ended with how Nigeria would fail if the south west pulls out.

My father wanted me to know about the Yoruba culture, and it had nothing to do with understanding my roots or finding myself, it was more about making me feel that like the culture I came from was better than all the others in Nigeria. Even after the civil war which happened before my mother was born, I and everyone around my age had elders in our lives who were constantly trying to recruit us into some kind of ethnic war, a silent resentment which they have been harboring for generations.

The bus ride to Ibadan was uncomfortable, Tola hadn't exactly said anything to me since his return from Oluchi's place, this made me assume Temi might have said something to him, but our very loud silence came to an end when we saw the prayer ground of a religious sect, the leader , Guru Tesbil, was notorious for being the topic of many outrageous rumors, there were stories of the leader claiming to be the reincarnation of Jesus, although I never met anyone who saw him claim he was, they were always passing down stories which were pass on to them.

It was also believed he uses the power of the devil to perform miracles, he wasn't the only religious leader that Nigerians were skeptical about, before him, there was another man who claimed to be Jesus, he was called *jesu* Ikeja 'Jesus of Ikeja'.

In this part of the world, people tend to pass on the responsibility for their life to some higher being, anytime they are face with an unsettling situation, they turn to a god instead of looking for a solution, this had made a lot of people vulnerable to people who claimed to have some sort of spiritual calling or power.

I grew up learning to look down on people who followed questionable faiths, people who didn't practice civilized Christianity. The grownups around me would scoff at people who walked on their bare feet and share stories about how a pastor made members of his church eat grass claiming it was manner from heaven, there were also stories about how another pastor made females of his church give him blow jobs saying his semen was the milk of the holy spirit. Anyone who didn't practice orthodox and Pentecostal Christianity were assumed to be involved in something diabolical, but they fail to realize how their own faith had obstructed them from thinking rationally and turned them into Zombies, for example Morenike's parents, they didn't eat grass or drink semen, but broke their children all in the name of religion.

Religion was what drove people, it was what gave them hope, and the peddlers of these beliefs were placed on the same pedestal as God himself.

Tola nudged me to look at the massive prayer ground , we laughed about the rumors we heard growing up and how our parents and friends were scared of everyone who followed this man's teaching, we even joked about Guru Tesbil using his super natural powers to hear us laughing at his faith.

For the first time during this trip Tola and I began to talk, mostly about Guru Tesbil and I didn't worry about Morenike who I had called after the night with Temi, I had told her I knew long distance could be hard but I was willing to try and if we would spend one day together and she still felt the same way about us being apart then I would stay away.

I felt going to see her would be me making an effort, after all, Ibadan wasn't that far from Lagos, it was a 2 hour drive and I could be there and right back in Lagos in no time considering there wasn't any traffic but I was leaving from Lagos the 2 hours most times turns to 4 but it was a sacrifice I was glad to make.

"hope you're holding a condom?" Tola asked dragging me away from my thoughts

"*err*, no"

"you want to end up being *baba* baby *abi*?"

I laughed because he had brought a thought I had been trying to suppress, I wasn't going to visit Morenike for sex but I had hoped that when I got there and everything was set we would, I don't know make up for the times I failed to kiss her

"what do you mean?" I said being sarcastic

"be doing as if you are not going to fuck that girl"

"try to lie to me that you don't want to"

"it's not that I will not if she wants me to, but that's not why I am going there actually, I really like her"

"be *yarning dust* there, better look for where to buy condom when we get down"

"okay *oo*" I chuckled "by the way Tola, where are you going to stay when we get there?"

"I am going to mark register with a *peng ting*" he said with a mischievous grin

"what of Oluchi?" I said in amusement

"what she doesn't know won't kill her"

I tried to reply Tola but I felt this surged of heavy mass dropping inside me, I began to feel dizzy, I was also feeling lightweight, it was like something was about to come out of me, I realized I couldn't hear sound except for the wind, I turned to Tola and saw he was falling fast asleep and so were all the other people on the bus except the driver, My eyes began to close, I tried hard not to fall asleep, my heart was beating hard and fast, it felt like it was going to cut free off my chest, my breathing was starting to become heavy, I looked towards the driver and it was the Ghanaian man, the man who had been stalking me, he wasn't there when I boarded the bus, how he got in I don't know, where the driver was, I had no idea either.

I was trying to catch my breath when an image of Guru Tesbil watching me through a mirror flashed before my eyes

"you are coming to us" the Ghanaian man said.

I woke up feeling this terrible itch all over my body, my eyes were too heavy to open, I was lying on the ground, and the rest of the world felt so distant.

"wake up! wake up!" a man shouted , but it sounded like his voice was coming from a muffled speaker

"wake up! wake up!" the man continued and my body jolted

"everybody get up now!!" the man's voice was so harsh and clear that it pierced through my subconscious and lifted the weight off my eyelids.

First, everything was covered by a thick fog, but slowly everything began to clear, I could see the Ghanaian man with two other men, one was elderly and had a white cloth wrapped around him, a few inches below his left eye was a mark the shape of a crescent moon which seemed to be made by some sort of white powder. He stepped forward with a white roaster and started chanting in what sounded like Yoruba but I couldn't understand, He raised the white roaster up, circled it in the air three times and then slit it's throat.

"Jesus!!! greater is he that is in me than he that is in the world, show yourself lord, no weapon fashioned against any of us shall prosper, father none of us shall be used for ritual...." the woman beside me kept screaming and this made me more awake and alert than ever. I realized that my right hand was chained to hers and my left hand was chained to man at my left hand side, I also realized that everyone was chained to someone.

This was what you see in movies and hear in church testimonies, when they talked about ritual killings in Nigeria, it always felt so distant, something that sounded like a myth, but you never dared to doubt if it was true or wasn't.

"shut up!" The Ghanaian man said pulling her forcefully which caused the rest of us serious pain because of the linking of our chains. the youngest of our abductors who looked like he was trying not to laugh, walked up to us, released the praying woman, and immediately, I saw the hole that was dug, it looked about 5 feet deep, there wasn't a way I could be sure, but what happened next gave me an idea of an estimate,

"Let see if Jesus can save you now" the Ghanaian man said as the old man which I supposed was the witch doctor started chanting again, both men dragged the woman to the hole, forced her into it and buried her in a standing position, they filled the hole with sand till it was just her head and shoulder which stuck out. The woman still wailing and crying kept saying "father forgive me, father forgive me" "father take care of my children, my children!"

"Let's see if your god will save you now", the Ghanaian man signaled the young man to move towards the woman with his cutlass, I struggled to take my eyes away but they wouldn't obey , it was like I had lost control of my face, the man swung his cutlass against the woman's neck but her head didn't come off, her blood started shooting out like water from a busted pipe, I could see the woman visibly fight for air, the man swung his cutlass against her neck, he kept swinging at it multiple times until her head came off and this brought a smile on his face.

Now the smell of urine was pungent, I looked around trying to find the culprit, that was when I realized that I couldn't see Tola anywhere, where did he go? did he find a way to escape? or was he killed before I woke up?

"I told you, you were going to come to us" the Ghanaian man said with a smirk on his face, and something weird happened after, the man with the cutlass started shape shifting into the policeman I met at the ATM who also said the words "you will come to us".

my head started spinning.

"she was leaving her husband's house" the man beside me said, I had not fully noticed him since I opened my eyes, I was only aware that my other hand was chained to a male figure. Now paying attention to all the captives, we were 6 in total minus the headless woman, her body was left there for us to watch, I don't know exactly why, maybe it was there as a reminder that we have been forsaken by God.

"she dropped her children with her sister and wanted to rest in Ibadan for a while before going to Port Harcourt"

"how do you know all these" I said with irritation , because with everything that was happening at that moment this man was more concerned about the headless woman's life.

"we live in the same area, her husband is a good friend of mine, we got on the bus together because I am a good Samaritan and I didn't want to look at her character, I don't know why women now-a-days don't like to listen to their husbands, this is what happens, *shey* you can see"

"but you are here too, is it because you did not listen to your wife? and I don't understand how being in the same bus with her makes you a good Samaritan"

"now watch it boy, don't be rude, we are all in this together, by the way if she had listened to her husband and not decided to be a career woman who was going to Port Harcourt and abandoning her children with her sister, she wouldn't be dead today"

"are you sure you know the full story?"

"of course yes"

" have you even tried to consider why a woman will want to leave her husband?" "she is irresponsible *ni*, its this feminism stuff that is wrong with all of them"

I wanted to argue more but I was too preoccupied with other stuffs, so I didn't respond and pretended I was falling asleep, that's when I smelt it again, the foul smell of hot urine and hot shit, I couldn't even get angry, we were all about to die, and your bowels will disgrace you in the face of danger. My body also came to the conclusion that this was the perfect time for it to betray me, I felt like vomiting, I fought the urge, trying not to mess the place more than it was already is, but my bowels started moving and this was followed by the stinging of my bladder which has suddenly become full, I felt like I was going to burst open and then did something I hadn't done in a while, I prayed to God not to let me die.

Chapter 6

I opened my eyes and felt a huge discomfort between my thighs, as I was coming into full consciousness with this banging headache, I realized I had soiled myself, feeling a mixture of disgust and comfort in my own mess, it came to my notice that I couldn't hear the voice of anybody, I was alone, I looked around and found myself in a different environment, and in my effort to be present, I saw it right in front of me, Morenike's grave stone, I was in a cemetery, and in front of me was the grave stone of the person I left Lagos to come and see, and on it was inscribed "in loving memory, Morenike Yewande Adekunbi, daughter and friend, 1997- 2017"

I spoke to Morenike immediately I was leaving Lagos, there was no way I could have slept for a year, there was no way I could have spoken and fallen in love with some that died in 2017 in 2018, how could she die? I love her, it just didn't add up, the tomb stone was already fading, the inscription had blended with the stone, and if Morenike had been dead for this long, who was I talking to all these while, who did I meet? who did I fall in love with? my head was now heavy and it was becoming impossible for my eyes socket to hold my eyes in, and then, everything became black.

"*werey ni?*" (a mad person) this words followed the rush of water that brought me back to consciousness, there were three people around me staring with disgust and curiosity, I rubbed my eyes trying to get a clear vision, the head ache was still there, I looked up

"who are you" I said squinting my eyes, still trying to get a clear vision of this people

"who are we? *abi* who are you, *ki lon she ni bi?*" (what are you doing here) an old grumpy looking man spat at me

" my name is... my name is..." I couldn't remember my name, how couldn't I remember my name, I was aware of who I was and fully aware of my memories but I just couldn't remember my name

"don't you know your name *ni?*" another said running out of patience "my name is Folarin" the words from my mouth shocked me myself, I knew my name wasn't Folarin, and I didn't know why I said it was,

"Folarin where are you from? and what are you doing here?" the old grumpy one asked again

"My name is Oluwole, my name is Oluwole, my name is Oluwole, my name is Oluwole!!!" I kept repeating my name, because I had found it and it belonged to me and I to it, I couldn't stop saying it, I couldn't stop calling for it, I was calling myself to me, I wasn't with them anymore, slightly elevated, I couldn't see anything

"*werey ni ooo, werey!!!*" (he is a mad person, he is mad) I heard them say and before I knew it, I was pinned down to the ground, and my hands were tied to my back with rough ropes which grazed my skin sharply

"*ki le le yi*" (what is this) someone said and yanked something that was glued to my skin, I felt a harsh sting

"if found please call this number" the person said and recited the number

The past few days has been a blur, between being at the graveyard and being here on this bed, it was hard telling what exactly was going when I just got here. And with that ugly blue ceiling staring down at me, I sat up to see what was in front of me and also to get a glimpse of my surrounding which was more confusing.

Right in front of me was a man bound to his bed, I am in a hospital bed but no one is hooked to a drip, instead there are people reading, chatting, laughing, but there are also odd things about this people I am packed in this room with, beside me, this middle age man was just staring to space and chatting with himself, he instantly reminded me of Iya Wande, this man was bound to his bed with a huge cover cloth when I first got here, he didn't struggle to break free, he didn't say anything, he didn't move, he just stared at the ceiling. I wondered what he could have done or who could have put him in that position, still trying to figure out exactly what was going on, a man who looked not far above 50 moved right to the middle of the room and defecated, The room erupted in disgust, and a group of people consisting of two women and a man rushed in the room dressed as nurses.

"Mr Alayode what have you done? no special lunch for you today" the youngest female nurse who seemed to be in her late teens or early twenties said as she tried to use her upper lip to cover her nostrils, the nurses cleaned the area and the male nurse took Mr Alayode to the toilet

"why are you people keeping me here ?!" I said with a tone that scratched my throat, the whole room fell silent and all eyes were on me, both female nurses came in and walked up to me

"do you know where you are?" the younger nurse said, I looked around me and then at her face before saying no, the other nurse who was slightly older nodded her head in pride like she wished to tell someone 'I told you so'

"are we in the day or in the night" the older nurse asked with an eagerness that was suspicious, I looked at her trying to figure out the motive behind her asking,

"day" I said in a bid to get their eyes off me

"it is time for socials and operational therapy" the male nurse said as he walked into the large room with Mr Alayode

"okay it's time for you to go" the youngest nurse said to me as they both motioned to leave me "where am I going to?"

"didn't you hear nurse Eniola *ni*"

"better do what they say if you want to leave here" a young man dressed like everyone in the room said with a smile on his face, he kept the smile and stared at me until it was uncomfortable to be on the receiving end of that smile.

I had to stand up and moved with the rest of my strange companions.

We got into a room that seemed like it used to be a very spacious cafeteria, there were more people like us, dressed in pajamas and flip flops, at different edges of the building, there were sewing machines, barbing clippers and other recreational stuffs scattered around the place.

I found myself a place to sit, that's when I really observed the pajamas I was in, I wondered whose it was but for some reason it felt oddly familiar, the mickey mouse smiley face and the softness of the fabric reminded me of a place I once called home.

"she killed a boy and his friend when they were trying to toast her" the guy with the weird smile said as he gestured to the girl who was sitting in front of me, the girl sat in a way that made me wonder how her muscles were able to hold her in that position, she didn't move, didn't talk to anyone, she just stared into space

"that's what ran her mad" the smiling guy continued,

"how do you know?" I responded disgusted

" I heard them when they were talking in her ward round, she was in a public transport, *danfo*, in Lagos traffic, that's when these boys pulled up beside the bus she was in, I think they were in an Uber, and the guy was trying to talk to her from the window, trying to get her number, and you know girls now, always trying to play hard to get even when they are on the main road, you know how Lagos is , one minute the traffic is on a stand still, the next minute everyone is driving like they have a death wish. In the process of this guys trying to keep pace with the bus while one of them tried to convince her to give him her number, they had an accident and railed off the EKO bridge".

I turned to him and asked "do you know why I am here?"

he looked at him and started laughing.

Chapter 7

You should know that I hate this place, it is filled with annoying routines, first we are forced to participate in the morning prayers, there isn't any consideration for those of us who might not be religious, and after that, there is the distributions of medications which always makes me drowsy and makes it hard for me to move my body. At first I thought about refusing, but the smiling psycho, Kelechi told me I would only make matters worse for myself, according to him, refusing the medications will result to me staying longer here, I have daily visits from people like you who claim to be doctors and other who called themselves social workers, they are all asking me intrusive questions at various intervals like you were about to before I started telling you my story, questions like where I was born, what my childhood was like, how was my first sexual encounter, if I ever did drugs, how was my family growing up, what jobs do my parents do. These questions are madly uncomfortable, but like the smiling psycho said, I have to do whatever I am asked if I want to get out of here.

I couldn't help but stare at the girl who killed the guys who were trying to toast her, every time I saw her, she was just staring into space, but there was this particular day she smiled and waved at me.

"do you think I am pretty or you just want to fuck me?" she said as she walked up to me

"*ehn*" I said looking confused

"don't try finding the political correct thing to say, you're in a mental hospital, a hospital for mad people, this is the only place you can be your true self, say your full mind and not be embarrassed or be scared of being judged, you already have an excuse, you are mad, and mad people get a pass for anything."

"so tell me, do you want to fuck me?" she continued

"first I am not mad and second you are scary" I said feeling terribly uncomfortable by the conversation

she busted into an hysterical laugh "so if you are not mad, then what are you doing here?"

"I don't know"

"the sooner you accept the truth the better for you"

"and what is the truth"

"the truth is, anyone you see here is mad even the doctors, psychologist, nurses and social workers."

"well I am not mad" I said getting irritated

"so why are you here?" she asked making it clear she didn't care if I was uncomfortable by the conversation

"I don't know"

she laughed again "you better know, if not, they won't allow you get out of here, you're a nuisance to the society and for you to get out you have to know why you are a nuisance"

"so you, why are you here" I shot back at her

she smiled at me " don't tell me you haven't heard the rumors"

"what rumors?"

"c'mon, what is your name *sef*"

"Wole. what is yours?"

"Wole I am Halima"

"so Wole, don't act like you haven't heard the rumors, I overheard you and your friend, well mostly your friend because he did most of the talking and you haven't stopped staring at me ever since"

"oh" I said feeling a bit of shame "so is it true that you killed them?"

"huh? is that how you processed the story? you must be really dump"

"*errm* I mean did they die because they were trying to toast you?"

she smiled and walked away, then she came back dragging my hand "today you are going to be my hand bag, you go where ever I go."

Words like hallucination and psychosis are becoming too familiar, people are being taken to what is called the psychology office to undergo psychological evaluation and this welcomed me into my new reality, the reality of being referred to as a patient, everyday patients are being taken into a room for what is called 'ward rounds', the nurses, doctors, psychologists like you and a whole lot of other people dressed in corporate clothing are constantly trying to save them from their madness, at first I did not understand how I got here, what must be going through Tola's mind, was he alive? what about my parents?, what of Morenike?, she must be worried sick and what was it about that gravestone, did I really see it, or was it just a dream, was I even at the grave? how the hell did I get here! these questions were laid heavy on my mind, Friday morning, the morning everything was laid out to me, the morning I was introduced to a more distressing reality.

"are you and Halima now a couple?" the smiling psycho Kelechi slammed himself on my bed interrupting my thoughts

"what?"

"you and Halima, are you guys going to make a madness baby?"

"what the hell are you talking about?"

"you don't know that madness is hereditary?"

"*ehn*"

"oh you don't know that your madness plus her madness is going to make a child with madness raised to power two"

"you have not even done ward rounds that's why you are looking lost, don't worry I think you are going to do ward rounds today"

"how do you know?"

"I just know stuffs" He smiled and walked away

Walking into my ward round that day was one of the hardest things I had to survive till date and that says a lot considering my story, I mean, I got into what seems like an office, and had this people all seated, claiming to be there for my wellbeing, then there was my parents and Tola, the site of Tola was the most distressing, how the hell did he survive? where had he been? how did he get here? how did my parents get here? how did they know where I was here?

"Tola how did you escape!" I said as I was unable to move to the seat which was set up for me, it wasn't like I had lost control of my foot, I just couldn't and I have no idea why

"escape from where?" Tola said looking confused

"how did you escape from the Guru Tesbil people who kidnapped us."

"when he first came he was claiming he was kidnapped and almost killed" one of the nurses said while every other person nodded. My mother was already shedding tears and my father who I had never seen show any sort of emotion except frustration and anger could be seen trying to hold himself from breaking down

"Wole please sit down" My mother said

"what are you guys doing here? how did you find me?"

"Wole your mother said sit down" my father chipped in, in all my 20 years in life there are a handful of moments where my parents were in agreement, and this was one of those rare moments, I had to obey, nothing signals the end of the world than my parents agreeing on something, especially when it comes to me.

I took my sit, in front of the doctors who sat opposite me , the eldest was the consultant and was joined with other junior doctors, they started smiling and one of them started reading what they called my case history.

" Wole is a 20 years old male of average height and no physical deformity, he was brought in account of talking to self, delusion and hallucination, he was brought by his parents who said they got a call saying he was found at the grave of his girlfriend covered in his own mess, his first episode of mental illness occurred at a party after taking substances such as cannabis and crack cocaine, there has also been reports of paranoid delusional beliefs, claiming he is being followed by a supposed Ghanaian man, recent episode was believed to have occurred when the patient stormed out of his house saying he was going to meet his dead girlfriend, all information were gotten from his parents and his best friend, client still has no insight into his illness and is mildly cooperative. we are querying Paranoid schizophrenia."

All the information was too much to take it, what did he mean by I was going to meet my dead girlfriend?

"Morenike is not dead, this one doesn't know what he is saying, Morenike is not dead, this one does not know what he is saying, Morenike is not dead this one does not know what he is saying" I kept repeating myself

"Wole but you saw her grave now, you saw she has been dead for over a year" the young doctor responded

"Morenike is not dead! Morenike is not dead! , I talked to her the day I got kidnapped, She is not dead!" I kept screaming at the top of my voice

The consultant stood up, "I'm sorry for upsetting you, lower your voice, I am sorry"

"Morenike is not dead, It is Yewande that should die she is the one that deserves to die"

"Yewande? Yewande is Morenike, everyone calls her Yewande, you the only one that calls her

Morenike, you said because it means 'I found someone to take care of' don't you remember" Tola said

I could feel the water in me rising and I was now finding it hard to breathe, I started rocking myself, and before I knew it I started shouting. This was an out of body experience, it felt like I was watching myself out of my body, my heart was experiencing so much ache it couldn't bare being in my body.

"okay that is enough for today" the consultant said and started stroking my back, now my father had broken down in tears, he had walked out of the room because he couldn't hold his wailing in, my mother was already a mess, and Tola was looking like a lost little boy

"Wole you can go to your bed now and relax, we will talk to you some other time" The consultant said as the nurse helped me to my bed after I was injected with something I suspect was a sedative.

Chapter 8

Please let me take some time to catch my breath, I know this might not mean much to you, but this isn't easy for me, for people to live they need two reasons, one a purpose, the other a reason, now I get the importance of religion, no matter how crazy the faith seems, it seems to give people some sort of purpose and reason to keep living, it might be the promise of eternal life or it might the illusion of some sort of success.

After everything that was said at my ward round, my purpose and reason left me, I see no reason why I need to open my eyes in the morning and before you write that I am suicidal in that your little book, I don't have the balls to kill myself, I have always been a coward, it was fear and lack of balls that prevented me from kissing Morenike when I had the chance.

I'm not even sure that even happened anymore, they are saying Morenike is not real or she is the same person as Yewande, but to me they are two different people.

You don't have an idea what it is like to wake up one morning and be told that your life is a lie, I am sure they didn't teach you that in your school, do you guys even know what you are doing? my life made sense until I got here, I knew what I was doing, who I was, now I don't know anymore.

The news of my melodramatic ward round had spread round the whole hospital, I know you probably heard of it before coming here, anyways the only thing that kept me afloat was Halima's company, she came to me during one of our social and occupational therapy session, it was my first outing after my ward round, I had been in bed for three days and was forced to eat during those periods. Nurse Eniola had tricked me into getting out of my bed saying she wanted to clean the bedsheet, only for her to take my bed hostage and tell me to come get it back after the social and occupational therapy, Kelechi had urged me to go along with the plan so as not to cause trouble for myself.

I positioned myself at a corner determined not to participate in anything, going home didn't make sense to me anymore because I had no idea what I will be going home to

"so how does it feel to be famous" Halima said interrupting my thought

"this is not the time" I said paying her no attention

"*omo how you go just lash out like that*"

I looked at her for a while, not sure what I was going to say or if I should even say anything

"you really loved that babe *huh*"

"yes"

"*omo* which kind of love is that, love that ran you mad"

"Halima why are you here"

"okay, sorry, I am sorry for your loss"

"she is not dead"

"oh baby, open your eyes, who did you think you saw at the grave yard"

"she is not dead"

Halima started laughing "at least now you can accept that you are mad like the rest of us"

"she is not dead! she is not dead! she is not dead!" I started shouting

"baba keep your voice down, she might not be dead to you but she is dead to everyone else, that is what being mad is all about, you have a different reality from everybody, to the world she has been dead for over a year and to you she might have just fucked you yesterday night"

"what is going on here," a nurse walked up to us

"nothing" Halima said

"Wole" the nurse looked at me

"nothing" I said as I watched the nurse walk away

"so what am I supposed to do now?" I turned to Halima

"accept your madness, Life is easier that way".

I am hearing that I might get to stay here for about 6 months, something about getting rid of my psychosis before going for drug treatments, you guys will just wake up one morning an decide to diagnose people using big words, anyway I will stay here as long as you guys want, So back to my story, I know you didn't sign up for this much information but I was on my bed, it was you who came to disturb my sleep and I am talking to you because there is something about you that reminds me of someone from another life.

My days are now between naps and getting drugged up, I don't do anything, I started having some side effects like over salivating and there was something about my walk that is funny, it is I am just learning to walk.

I want to ask you something? do you think you guys are doing the right thing by trying to make us better? do you really feel reality is better than delusion? I mean look at the world, there is hunger, there are deaths, there are diseases, there is hate, there is pain, there is loss, and our mind which I feel is doing what it was made to do, creates an alternate reality what you guys call delusion as a form of self preservation from the trauma and chaos of the world, you think you know and decide to take us out of the solace of our alternate reality and force us into the reality of the world.

Before I came here, I was in love with someone, I was happy, I know there might be some set backs here and there, but there was promise everything was going to be alright, I loved Morenike and we were going to be together, she was my someone to care for, now you guys come with your drugs, suits and books and tell me she is dead and I have to accept it just like that.

Tola came to visit me separately, and my past got more weird

"Tola please tell me everything" I had asked

" everything as in how?"

"what happened? how did I get here?"

"After that day when you came home telling us about the Ghanaian man, you started acting strange, saying the man was following you around, we first thought it was a joke until the day we decided to just drink and chill" "the day you left me and Temi to go to Oluchi's house?"

"I did not go to Oluchi's house, Oluchi was there with us"

You see, like I have said, this is very hard for me, it is had to accept, it is hard to take in, it felt like I was being erased and re written, like I wasn't in control of my own story and for me to know about myself I have to ask someone else

"it was the day you kissed Temi and brought out your dick and tried to force her to suck it" Tola continued

"did she vomit?" I asked this question hoping that something from my reality happened for real

"yes she did, and after that you kept screaming, how will I tell Tola, I have betrayed Tola, you were shouting the same way you shouted at your ward rounds"

And no I did not ask about the death of Morenike, at least not yet, all I had listened to was too much for one day, I remember standing up without even saying goodbye and went to sleep, because sleep was the only place I could find solace from this oppressive reality.

Chapter 9

I should be getting to the end of my story, I know you must be tired, I am tired as well, but I still can't figure out what it is about you that's making me talk, the doctors, nurses and psychologists have been trying to get words out of me but to no avail, they treat me like a child who doesn't know anything and I am not ready to give them the satisfaction of accepting that I have a flawed reality.

You remind of this guy who when I was in UNI left his diary for his twin sister before he went to get himself killed, I used to admire him from afar, I never shared this with my friends, I went to a show he was DJing once and he got booed off, he wasn't bad, I loved his set, but you know Nigerians are a tough crowd. He witnessed the death of someone, if you attended Unilag you will know about it, anyways the people who were present at the killing of that individual tried to shut him up but I don't know why he decided to go after them, I never got to read the diary, only his twin had access to it, all this information are based off rumors.

His name was Folarin, I think he was the one that came to my mind at the graveyard, I wanted to be him, he was comfortable in his lonely, while I constantly mess myself up seeking validation from everything and everyone.

You look like him, the warmth in your eyes and I think I am talking to you because before he died, I always wanted to talk to him but never summed up the courage to, and since I am messed up in the head, I can pretend that he is you and you are him.

You know, Temi came to see me yesterday, it was the oddest thing, I had this surge of so much emotions but this time there wasn't any crazy outburst I think, Temi opened my eyes to everything, from love, to the journey that got me here, and boy was it a lot to take in

"why are you here" I asked as I walked into the visitors room

"I came to see you" she had a smile on her face

"how are you doing?" she asked

"are they treating you well?"

"yes" I responded

there was silence for a brief moment and then she said "Wole, Tola told me everything"

"yeah?"

"he said you lost your memory"

"I did not lose my memory, just seem to have seen everything that happened differently"

"things like what?"

" they said I tried to assault you, Tola said I tried to force you to suck my dick, but how I remember it, you came up to me offering a blowjob only for you to vomit all over mid way through the process"

"what?" she chuckled

"I'm sorry by the way"

"it's fine, I know that wasn't you, I have been reading a lot about stuffs like this"

"why were you always giving me grieve?"

"how do you mean"

"you're always making fun of me"

"you mean when we were young?"

"even has we grew older"

" I don't really think I did anything major, I just wished you would love me as much as you loved Yewande or Morenike like you call her. maybe not as intense though"

"The doctor brought their picture once and I felt really stupid"

"why?"

"I couldn't tell who was Yewande and who was Morenike"

"yes na, they are the same person"

"what really happened? how did she die?'

" you don't remember?" "not the slightest clue"

"it was the night after the party, you had smoked crack, I don't know who gave you that shit, but you went in the mist of everyone, stripped naked and started dry humping some girl"

" which girl?" "me"

"why am I always getting naked in front of you" "I should ask you" she said laughing

"so she didn't cheat on me?"

"No she didn't but she thought you cheated on her, she walked in on you dry humping me and stormed off"

"do you know if she ever called back telling me how immature I am?"

"no she didn't, that was when she died, she had an accident just immediately after she left the house, but she called you immature all the time"

For a minute there I found it hard to breathe, my head began to spin, then I had my mild blackout, my vision went black and within seconds everything came back to normal, but I could remember the scene, I could remember Yewande, I could remember Morenike, I started crying and hyperventilating, I remember the call from the hospital and how her Uncle had preventing me from attending her funeral, claiming I led her straight to her death.

"are you okay? should I call someone" Temi walked up to me confused about what to do

"no please don't, let me just catch my breath"

"okay" she said as she watched me like a hawk.

"tell me about Oluchi"

"what about her?"

" I'm not crazy to not like her"

" so you still haven't gotten over that?"

" over what?"

"her choosing Tola over you?"

"Oh, shit, I'm really chaotic when it comes to girls"

"she had been gumming up to you only for her to leave you for my brother"

"but we were always fighting"

"you and Oluchi?"

There is nothing Romantic about death by Banji Coker

"no *jor*, I mean Morenike and I"

"well yeah, but which couple didn't, you guys were intense and obsessive, you guys had the kind of love that turned people into serial killers and when you didn't react to her death, you didn't even cry, it was a huge surprise to all of us, it was even scary, we were all holding our breaths only for all of this to happen a year later".

"why now, why is everything happening now?"

"I don't know, but you guys had a plan to go to Ghana and start a life together away from your parents and her uncle"

"and we were supposed work for a year, save money and relocate, the day I met the Ghanaian man was the day we were supposed to leave to Ghana.

"yes you remember, and also the day you ended up at her gravestone, was you guys anniversary"

"Pain demands to be felt right?"

"yeah, pain demands to be felt"

"how do you even know about our anniversary, you know an awful amount of information about my relationship with her"

"I love you Wole, I have always loved you, your relationship was my business and I would cry every night, it was her seeing you love her the way you did"

"wole"

"wole"

"wole"

I can't remember what happened next, I think I passed out and when I opened my eyes, Temi had already gone, but there still a part of me that doubts if what happened yesterday was real, I mean I am a mad person.

About the Author

Banji Coker is a Nigerian writer, poet and a spoken word artist, his first poetry compilation, October feelings was published in 2016, which was incidentally followed by another poetry compilation, Just Seventeen in 2017. He was nominated for the best student poet category in the 2017 SWAAP awards. He released a spoken album, If you see me liking a girl, shoot me, in march of 2020.

Milton Keynes UK
Ingram Content Group UK Ltd.
UKHW040638131123
432470UK00001B/151